SPACE · SCIENCE

Eclipses

Jessica Morrison
and Steve Goldsworthy

MEDIA ENHANCED BOOKS
AV2 BY WEIGL™
ADDED VALUE · AUDIO VISUAL

www.av2books.com

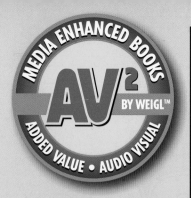

AV² provides enriched content that supplements and complements this book
Weigl's AV² books strive to create inspired learning and engage young mind
in a total learning experience.

Your AV² Media Enhanced books come alive with...

Audio
Listen to sections of
the book read aloud.

Key Words
Study vocabulary, and
complete a matching
word activity.

Go to **www.av2books.com**,
and enter this book's
unique code.

Video
Watch informative
video clips.

Quizzes
Test your knowledge.

BOOK CODE

B 2 2 8 1 6 5

Embedded Weblinks
Gain additional information
for research.

Slide Show
View images and
captions, and prepare
a presentation.

AV² by Weigl brings you media
enhanced books that support
active learning.

Try This!
Complete activities and
hands-on experiments.

... and much, much more!

Published by AV² by Weigl
350 5th Avenue, 59th Floor
New York, NY 10118

Website: www.weigl.com   www.av2books.com
Copyright ©2012 AV² by Weigl

Library of Congress Cataloging-in-Publication Data

Morrison, Jessica.
Eclipses / Jessica Morrison.
    p. cm. -- (Space science)
Includes index.
ISBN 978-1-61690-631-3 (hardcover : alk. paper) -- ISBN 978-1-61690-635-1 (softcover : alk. paper)
1. Eclipses--Juvenile literature. I. Title.
QB175.M67 2012
523.9'9--dc22

                              2010050411

Printed in North Mankato, in the United States of America
1 2 3 4 5 6 7 8 9 0   13 12 11 10 09

062011
WEP290411

Weigl would like to acknowledge Getty Images and NASA as its primary photo suppliers for this title.

SENIOR EDITOR: Heather Kissock
ART DIRECTOR: Terry Paulhus

Eclipses

CONTENTS

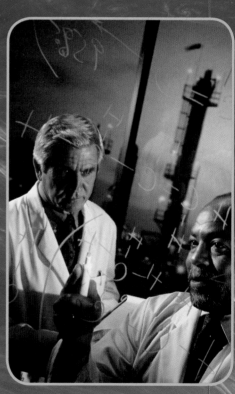

What Is an Eclipse?

An eclipse occurs when one object moves in front of another, hiding it from view. When a person wears a hat with a large brim to shield his or her eyes, the brim eclipses the Sun. Eclipses can also happen on a much larger scale. Many people are fascinated by these larger eclipses.

In **astronomy**, an eclipse occurs when all or part of one **celestial body** is behind another one and is in its shadow. Most commonly, three celestial bodies, such as the Sun, the Moon, and Earth, are in line. In the past, many people became frightened when an eclipse occurred. It can appear **ominous** for the Sun or Moon to be covered by a shadow. All eclipses, however, can be explained with science.

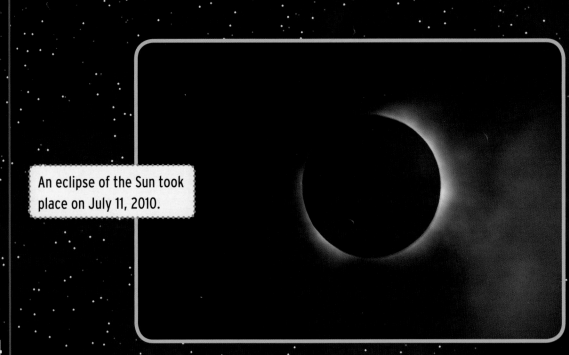

An eclipse of the Sun took place on July 11, 2010.

4

Scientists in Spain viewed an eclipse in 1870.

An eclipse can look dramatic in the night sky. Occasionally, people in Washington, D.C., can observe an eclipse and the brightly lit Washington Monument at the same time.

BRAIN BOOSTER

The ancient Maya feared that an eclipse would lead to the end of the world. They prayed to the Sun God Ah-Kin Chob to battle the darkness and restore the sunshine.

Many American Indian tribes believed the Sun lost its fire when an eclipse occurred. They would shoot flaming arrows into the sky to bring back the Sun's powers.

Orbits and Eclipses

Eclipses occur because celestial bodies are in motion. Some of them orbit, or travel around, another celestial body. Earth orbits the Sun, and the Moon orbits Earth. They travel in curved paths that are shaped like ovals. Earth takes one year to go around the Sun once. The Moon takes about a month to go once around Earth.

As Earth and the Moon travel in their orbits, at times the Moon passes between Earth and the Sun. When this happens, the Moon blocks sunlight from reaching a part of Earth for a short time. It casts a shadow on Earth. For people in this shadow, the Sun appears to be covered, and daylight may briefly turn into darkness. This event is called a **solar eclipse**.

At other times as Earth and the Moon orbit, Earth passes between the Sun and the Moon. Earth briefly blocks sunlight from reaching the Moon. This event is called a **lunar eclipse**.

Scientists today know the paths that Earth and the Moon take in their orbits. They know the speeds at which Earth and the Moon travel. Using this information, they can accurately predict the times and places at which eclipses will occur in the future.

Earth and the Moon's Orbits

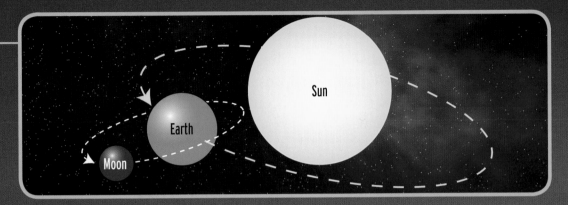

Solar Eclipse

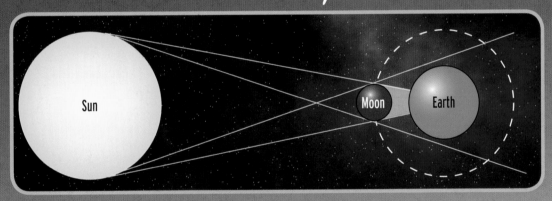

Lunar Eclipse

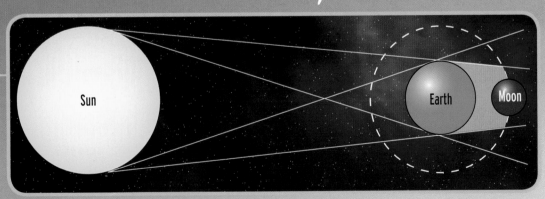

Solar
Eclipses

There are different types of solar eclipses. They include total eclipses, partial eclipses, and annular eclipses. The type of eclipse that occurs depends on the Moon's location in space.

In a total eclipse, the Sun appears to be completely covered. It looks like a black circle with only a thin halo of light around it. This halo is the region around the Sun called the **corona**. A total solar eclipse does not last for a long time. It is normally visible in any one spot for only about 3 minutes. A total eclipse occurs when Earth, the Moon, and the Sun are exactly aligned. In a total eclipse, the Moon's orbit takes it close to Earth. The Moon appears large enough to totally block the Sun in the sky.

A partial eclipse occurs when the Sun, the Moon, and Earth are almost but not exactly aligned. In a partial eclipse, only part of the Sun is covered by the Moon. The Sun appears to have a bite taken out of it.

A solar eclipse was visible in China in January 2010.

An annular eclipse happens when the Moon passes in front of the Sun but does not completely cover it. These eclipses occur when the Moon's orbit takes it far away from Earth. The Moon looks too small in the sky to completely cover the Sun. During an annular eclipse, a ring of sunlight surrounds the shadow of the Moon.

The shadow the Moon casts on Earth during an eclipse has two parts. They are the **umbra** and the **penumbra**, or complete and partial shadows. As the Moon travels between Earth and the Sun, the area of Earth that is completely blocked from sunlight at some time during this passage is called the **path of totality**. The path, which covers about one percent of Earth's surface area, is usually 10,000 miles (16,000 kilometers) long but only 100 miles (160 kilometers) wide. People in the path of totality are in the Moon's umbra. In areas outside but close to the path of totality, a partial solar eclipse occurs. These areas are in the Moon's penumbra.

An annular eclipse is sometimes called a "ring of fire" because a bright ring of sunlight can be seen during the event.

Lunar
Eclipses

Lunar eclipses occur during a full Moon, when the Moon usually looks like a complete circle of light in the night sky. These eclipses can be total or partial. In a total lunar eclipse, the Sun, Earth, and the Moon are aligned, and Earth's shadow completely covers the Moon. In a partial eclipse, they are almost aligned. Earth's shadow partly covers the Moon.

During a total lunar eclipse, the Moon does not become dark. It actually turns a reddish-orange color. This happens because some of the Sun's light still reaches the Moon even though it is completely within Earth's shadow.

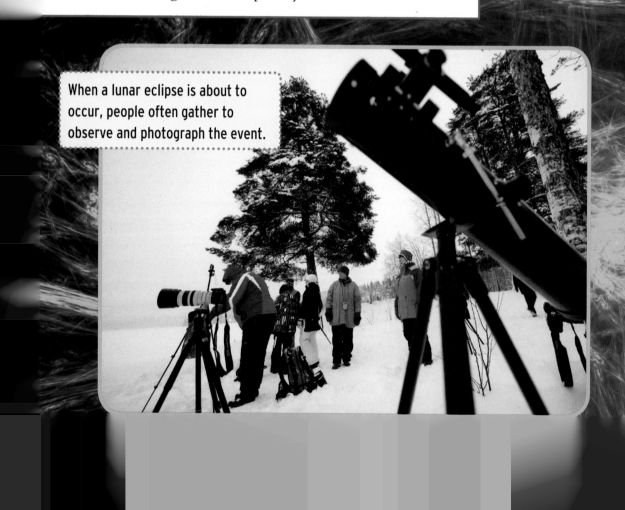

When a lunar eclipse is about to occur, people often gather to observe and photograph the event.

Sunlight is made up of different kinds of light that have various colors, including blue, red, and yellow. Some sunlight traveling past Earth during a lunar eclipse goes through Earth's **atmosphere**, the ring of air around the planet. During this passage through the atmosphere, the sunlight is separated into its different colors. The atmosphere acts like a lens and bends the rays of red light. It is the same effect that produces reddish colors during a sunset. As the red light is bent, some of it reaches the Moon while it is in Earth's shadow. The result is the reddish color viewers can see during a total lunar eclipse.

The Moon can turn a wide range of reddish colors during a lunar eclipse. It might look pink, copper, or bright red.

THINK ABOUT IT
If Earth had no atmosphere, the Moon would be completely black instead of red during a total lunar eclipse. Why do you think this might be?

Eclipses in History

Sunlight and moonlight have always been Earth's major sources of natural light. Some ancient civilizations were terrified when one of these light sources seemed to disappear. There were many **mythological** explanations for eclipses. The Inuit believed eclipses were evil omens. Ancient Norse tribes thought that a wolf named Sköll was eating the Sun during an eclipse. In many cultures, people would gather together to make noise during an eclipse by screaming or banging drums. They believed the noise scared the evil away.

Scientific study of eclipses is also thousands of years old. Scientists in ancient China, for example, noticed a pattern in their occurrence. By studying records of when eclipses had occurred, these scientists were able to predict future eclipses. The oldest eclipse records from China are more than 4,000 years old.

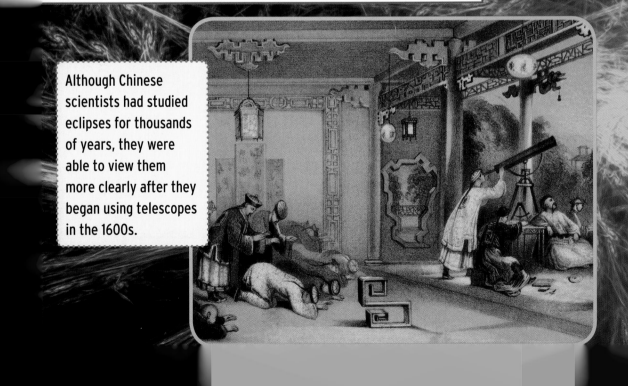

Although Chinese scientists had studied eclipses for thousands of years, they were able to view them more clearly after they began using telescopes in the 1600s.

The prehistoric monument Stonehenge, in England, was constructed between 2800 BC and 1500 BC. Some historians think it was used for predicting eclipses. Little is known about the people who built the monument, but researchers have found patterns in the stones that suggest they were used to track the occurrence of eclipses.

The stones used in England's Stonehenge monument weigh as much as 8,000 pounds (3,600 kilograms).

THINK ABOUT IT

Scientist believe some of the stones at Stonehenge were moved hundreds of miles (kilometers) to the monument's site. How were the ancient people who built the monument able to move heavy stones such long distances without modern machinery?

Eclipse Experts

Humans have been fascinated by celestial objects and events for centuries. Today, many countries have space exploration agencies to study them. The National Aeronautics and Space Administration, or NASA, was established in 1958. NASA is the United States' leading space exploration agency.

NASA keeps records of the date, time, location, and length of every type of eclipse that occurs. This information is available to the public online. The NASA Eclipse Bulletin contains predictions and maps for future solar eclipses. People interested in eclipses can sign up online to receive copies of this bulletin. The NASA website also gives advice on eclipse photography, ways to build eclipse viewers, and how to find eye protection for safely viewing eclipses.

> Detailed information about recent eclipses, including maps showing where they could be seen, is available on NASA's website.

Annular Eclipse
2010 Jan 15

Saros 141

Mag. = 0.919
Gam. = 0.400

Alt. = 66°
Dur. = 11^m 08^s

> NASA does many things besides studying eclipses. One of its best-known achievements was landing the first person on the Moon in 1969.

Other Kinds of Eclipses

Not every eclipse involves the Sun, Earth, and Moon. Sometimes, the planet Mercury or Venus, while orbiting the Sun, will pass in front of the Sun as seen from Earth. This type of eclipse is called a **planetary transit**. As a transit occurs, the planet is visible as a tiny dot traveling over the Sun's face. Planetary transits are rare. There are about 13 transits of Mercury every one hundred years. Transits of Venus generally happen in pairs, with eight years between the two. Then, more than a century usually passes before the next Venus transit pair begins.

The last Mercury transit occurred in 2006. The next will occur in 2013.

Mercury is the closest planet to the Sun. It is about 36 million miles (58 million kilometers) away. The second-closest is Venus, about 67 million miles (108 million kilometers) from the Sun. Next is Earth, at about 93 million miles (150 million kilometers).

BRAIN BOOSTER

Artificial
Eclipses

The Sun is just one of billions of stars in the universe. It is very important to humans, however, because it is the closest to Earth. It is Earth's source of heat, and it controls the planet's climate.

Only the Sun's outer layers, which are called the solar atmosphere, can be seen. There are three parts of the solar atmosphere. They are the photosphere, the chromosphere, and the corona. The corona, which is the outermost section of the atmosphere, is visible only during a total solar eclipse. At other times, other areas of the Sun are too bright for the corona to be seen from Earth.

Scientists are interested in studying the corona in order to learn more about the Sun. In the past, they needed to wait for an eclipse to view it. Today, there is an instrument called a coronagraph that can mimic an eclipse. A coronagraph is an attachment for a telescope that blocks out the direct light from a star. When it is used on the Sun, it allows scientists to view the corona.

The coronagraph was invented by a French astronomer named Bernard Lyot.

Coronagraphs also allow scientists to view the Sun's prominences. Prominences, also known as filaments, are dense clouds of material that extend into the corona. They are often in the shape of a loop and usually extend for thousands of miles. The longest prominence on record was estimated to be more than 430,000 miles (692,000 kilometers) long. Scientists are currently trying to figure out exactly how and why prominences are formed.

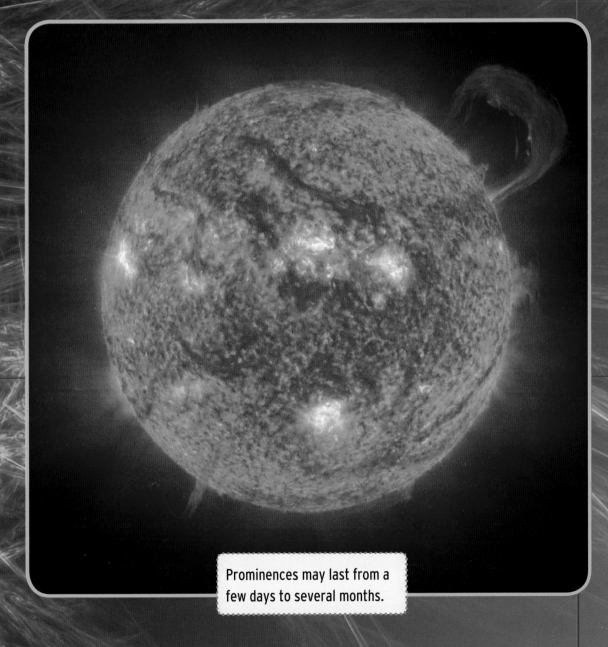

Prominences may last from a few days to several months.

Help
from Eclipses

Scientists have gathered a great deal of valuable information by studying solar eclipses. Some of this information has enabled scientists to better predict when solar flares will occur. Solar flares are explosions in the Sun's atmosphere. The flares can reach Earth and cause damage.

Scientists have learned more about solar flares by studying eclipses. Sometimes, scientists change the colors in a picture to help them see a solar flare more clearly.

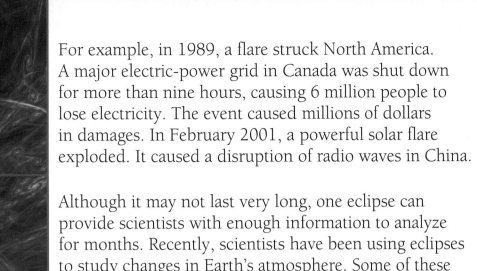

For example, in 1989, a flare struck North America. A major electric-power grid in Canada was shut down for more than nine hours, causing 6 million people to lose electricity. The event caused millions of dollars in damages. In February 2001, a powerful solar flare exploded. It caused a disruption of radio waves in China.

Although it may not last very long, one eclipse can provide scientists with enough information to analyze for months. Recently, scientists have been using eclipses to study changes in Earth's atmosphere. Some of these changes affect Earth's climate. The brightness of a lunar eclipse may give clues about chemicals in the atmosphere. By studying how light reaching the Moon in a lunar eclipse now may be different from light reaching the Moon in the past, scientists can determine how Earth's atmosphere may have changed over time.

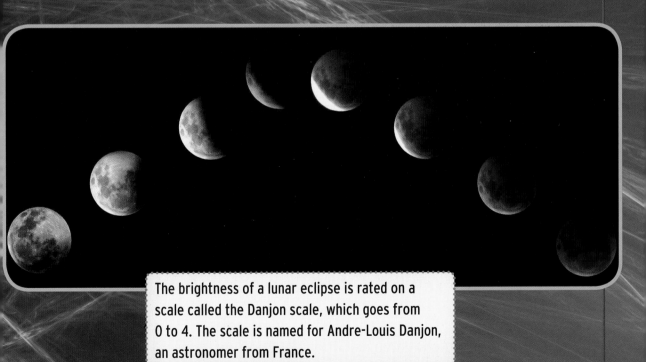

The brightness of a lunar eclipse is rated on a scale called the Danjon scale, which goes from 0 to 4. The scale is named for Andre-Louis Danjon, an astronomer from France.

The Study of
Space

By studying and observing eclipses, humans learned about the relative positions of Earth, the Moon, and the Sun. There are many areas of science that have benefited from knowledge gained by studying eclipses.

Many ancient cultures developed devices called astrolabes to find and predict the location of the Sun, Moon, and planets. They were used to show how the sky looked from one place at a certain time. Astrolabes had moving parts that could be adjusted for time and dates. These instruments have sometimes been called "ancient computers."

The astrolabe was commonly used until about 1650, when it was replaced with more complicated instruments such as the sextant. A sextant can be used to measure the angle between any two objects. It is used, for example, to measure the angle of the Sun or another celestial body above the horizon. Once the angle and time of day are known, it is possible to determine one's location and navigate safely. Today, other types of navigation equipment, such as Global Positioning Systems, or GPS, also depend on knowledge of Earth's place in the cosmos.

Astrolabes were used for more than one thousand years before the invention of the sextant.

Mr. Eclipse

Fred Espenak is a retired astrophysicist who worked as an eclipse specialist for NASA. He is thought to be one of the world's leading eclipse experts. Born in 1953, Espenak became interested in astronomy and eclipses when he was a young man. Over the years, he has observed more than 20 eclipses in person. He has traveled all over the world in order view them.

During his career at NASA, Espenak published yearly eclipse bulletins for scientists and other space enthusiasts. The bulletins provided eclipse viewers with detailed information about where and when every eclipse of the year would occur. He has also published several books about eclipses and is one of the world's leading eclipse photographers.

THINK ABOUT IT

Fred Espenak's interest in eclipses began when he witnessed a total solar eclipse in March 1970. Have you ever seen an eclipse? When is the next eclipse in your area?

Eclipses from
Space

Sometimes, it is possible for astronauts in space to view a solar eclipse from their space vehicle. This provides them with a rare view of the event. They can watch from above as parts of Earth become dark. In order to view an eclipse, an astronaut must be over the right portion of Earth. Since eclipses last for only a short period of time, an astronaut must prepare in advance to be ready to observe and possibly take photographs of the event.

A lunar eclipse occurred over the space shuttle *Discovery* while it was on the ground before a launch at the Kennedy Space Center in Florida in 2010.

Just as people on Earth must often travel to experience an eclipse, so must astronauts. In 1966, one of NASA's *Gemini* missions changed its course in order to view a solar eclipse over the eastern Pacific Ocean. Viewing eclipses from space became somewhat easier once astronauts began to live in space stations for extended periods of time. For example, in 1999, the crew of Russia's *Mir* space station watched as an eclipse spread over Europe.

Today, astronauts from many countries are spending long periods of time in space aboard the International Space Station, or ISS. The ISS is the largest artificial satellite that has ever orbited Earth. Over time, astronauts on the ISS will have a number of chances to view eclipses. The information and photographs sent back to Earth will help scientists who study eclipses learn more about these events and the celestial bodies that cause them.

Photographs taken from the International Space Station show the Moon's shadow covering part of Earth during a solar eclipse.

GET CONNECTED

To learn more about the International Space Station, go to http://www.nasa.gov/mission_pages/station/main/index.html.

Careers in
Astronomy

Studying eclipses and other astronomical events requires people to have very specific skills and knowledge. Specialists in many different branches of astronomy examine eclipses. They all need to use science and math.

ASTROMETRIST

By observing and analyzing eclipses, it is possible to examine the features of different celestial bodies. Astrometry is a specialized branch of astronomy. Astrometrists measure the distances and motions of celestial bodies, including planets and stars. People who become astrometrists often like to work with detailed information. They must be patient enough to gather data and study a question over a long period of time. They usually study astronomy and mathematics in high school and college, and they may specialize in astrometry in their later education.

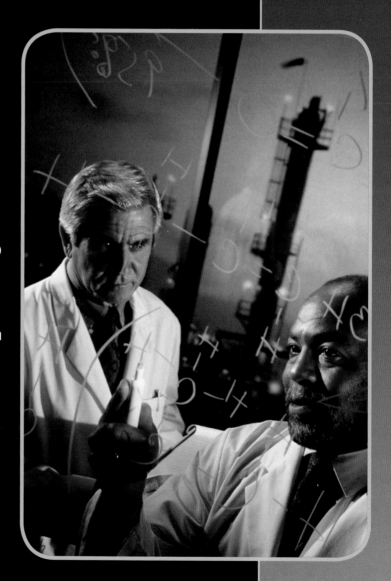

ASTROPHOTOGRAPHER

An astrophotographer's job is to document celestial events using photography. Astrophotography requires not only a background in general photography, but also the skills needed to use specialized equipment. Telescopes, high-powered lenses, and advanced

digital camera equipment are necessary to capture detailed images of astronomical events. It is also essential to have a knowledge of astronomy. Many of the photos taken by astrophotographers are studied by scientists in order to better understand astronomical events. Most astrophotographers are creative and energetic. They study photography in school, with special attention to techniques for night-time photography and capturing astronomical images.

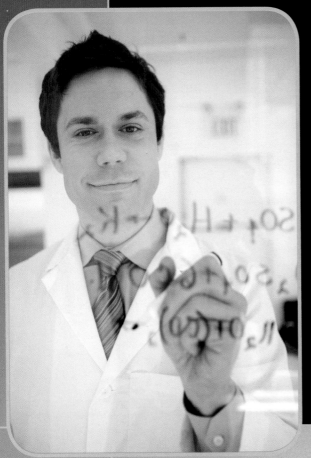

ASTROPHYSICIST

An astrophysicist is an astronomer who specializes in physics. Physics is the science of matter and energy. Astrophysicists study the physics of the universe. They might investigate the physical properties of a celestial body such as a star or a planet, or learn more about how stars form and change. Some astrophysicists research topics such as the origin of the universe or the possibility of life on other planets. People in this field usually have a bachelor's degree and a graduate degree in some area of math or science.

Viewing
Eclipses

It is easy to observe a total lunar eclipse. As Earth passes in front of the Moon, the viewer will slowly see the Moon turn reddish-orange. It is more difficult to watch a solar eclipse. In order to view a total solar eclipse, a person must be at just the right place on Earth. During any solar eclipse, the Moon's path of totality will cover only part of the planet. A total solar eclipse is visible somewhere on Earth about every 18 months. However, an eclipse will occur in the same place, on average, only about once every 370 years.

People must be very careful when observing a solar eclipse. Looking directly at the Sun during a solar eclipse can cause permanent eye damage and even blindness. A solar eclipse can be safely observed by watching the ground. As the beams of sunshine hit the ground, viewers will see the light begin to fade. The Sun will become a shrinking crescent, and viewers will observe more and more darkness at their feet.

People interested in eclipses often photograph the crescent of light the Sun makes on the ground as an eclipse is beginning.

Another safe way to watch a solar eclipse is to view it indirectly using a piece of cardboard. Viewers can cut a small hole in the cardboard and set the cardboard on a window sill, letting the sunlight shine through the hole onto a wall of a room. As the eclipse occurs, the light on the wall will act as a miniature Sun. Viewers will see the eclipse on the wall.

It is also possible to buy eye-protection devices that are made to allow people to safely watch an eclipse directly. These devices usually have a thin layer of metal to reduce the intensity of the light. Eclipse viewers should not attempt to make eye-protection devices themselves and should never look directly at an eclipse unless they have proper equipment made for safe viewing.

Eye-protection devices used by eclipse watchers may have a sheet of aluminum, chromium, or silver to block some of the sunlight.

Test Your
Knowledge

1 What are three types of solar eclipse?

Partial eclipse, total eclipse, annular eclipse

2 What is the path of totality?

The part of Earth that can see a total solar eclipse

3 What is the halo of light around the Sun called?

The corona

4 What invention allowed scientists to study the Sun's corona without waiting for an eclipse?

The coronagraph

5 Which device was used by ancient cultures to find and predict the location of the Sun, Moon, and planets?

The astrolabe

6 What is the name of the U.S. government's leading space exploration agency?

The National Aeronautics and Space Administration, or NASA

7 Is it dangerous to look directly at a lunar eclipse?

No. It is only dangerous to look at a solar eclipse.

8 About how many transits of Mercury occur every hundred years?

13

9 What are the two parts of the shadow created during an eclipse?

The umbra and penumbra

10 What color does the Moon become during a lunar eclipse?

Red or orange

Glossary

astronomy: the study of planets, stars, and other objects in space

atmosphere: the layer of gases that surrounds a planet

celestial body: a natural object in space, such as a star or planet

corona: the outermost region of the Sun's atmosphere; this area is seen as a halo during a solar eclipse

lunar eclipse: an eclipse that occurs when Earth travels between the Moon and the Sun

mythological: imaginary

ominous: threatening

orbit: the path of a celestial body as it travels around another celestial body

path of totality: the path the Moon's shadow traces upon Earth during a total solar eclipse

penumbra: the shadow region outside an umbra

planetary transit: the passage of a planet in front of the Sun as viewed from Earth

solar eclipse: an eclipse that occurs when the Moon travels between Earth and the Sun

umbra: a region of complete shadow

Index

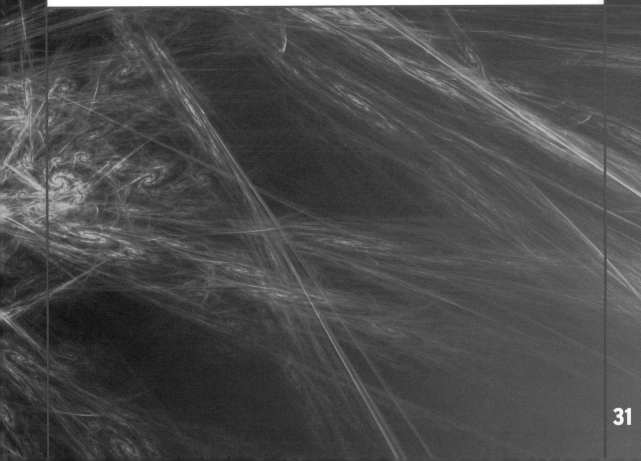

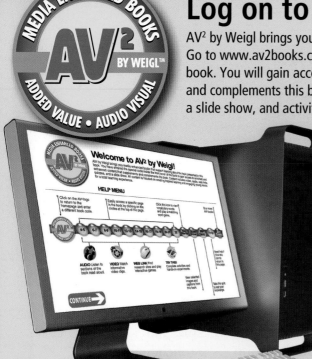

Log on to www.av2books.com

AV² by Weigl brings you media enhanced books that support active learning. Go to www.av2books.com, and enter the special code found on page 2 of this book. You will gain access to enriched and enhanced content that supplements and complements this book. Content includes video, audio, web links, quizzes, a slide show, and activities.

Audio
Listen to sections of the book read aloud.

Video
Watch informative video clips.

Embedded Weblinks
Gain additional information for research.

Try This!
Complete activities and hands-on experiments.

WHAT'S ONLINE?

Try This!	**Embedded Weblinks**	**Video**	**EXTRA FEATURES**
Complete engaging activities that further explain eclipses. Write a biography about an important person. Test your knowledge of space. Play a fun interactive activity.	Learn more about eclipses. Find out more about a notable person. Learn more about pursuing a career studying eclipses. Find out more about the technology used to study eclipses.	Watch a video about eclipses. Check out another video about eclipses.	**Audio** Listen to sections of the book read aloud. **Key Words** Study vocabulary, and complete a matching word activity. **Slide Show** View images and caption and prepare a presentati **Quizzes** Test your knowledge.

AV² was built to bridge the gap between print and digital. We encourage you to tell us what you like and what you want to see in the future.

Sign up to be an AV² Ambassador at www.av2books.com/ambassador.